Charlie's Boat

Lulu

Oliver

Charlie

Kit Chase

G. P. PUTNAM'S SONS

It was a fine fishing day.

"I caught a fish!"
said Oliver.

"Me too!"
squealed Lulu.

"I caught a stick,"
said Charlie.

Charlie caught a lot of sticks.
"I can't fish," he grumbled.
"All the fish are in the middle,
and the water's too
deep for me."

Charlie sat next to
the pile of sticks.

Suddenly, he had an idea.

"Watch this!"
Charlie shouted
to his friends.

"Wow! Let's all make boats!"
suggested Lulu.

So they poked and fiddled and twisted and tied
until their boats were just right.

Oliver made a
long, flat boat.

Lulu made a
small, little boat.

Charlie made a big, tall boat.

"My boat's the biggest and fastest!" said Charlie.

"There's only one way to find out," said Oliver.
"Let's have a race!"

Ready . . .

set . . .

GO!

Lulu's boat took off like a flash,
with Oliver's right behind.

Charlie's boat was big.
But it wasn't very fast.

It got stuck
on some rocks

and tangled in some branches.

When they got to the finish
line, Lulu's boat came in first,
Oliver's came in second,
and Charlie's finished
a very slow last.

"Congratulations," muttered Charlie.
He tried to be happy for his friends,
but he didn't feel very happy.
"I guess I'm not good at fishing or making boats."

"That's it!" cried Oliver.

"I've got a grand idea that will help you do both."

"Here, Charlie," said Oliver.
"Help me lash this stringy vine
to these logs."

"I know what to do with this,"
Lulu chirped.

When they were all finished, Lulu helped Oliver push his grand idea into the water, and they sent Charlie to gather their fishing supplies.

"Ahoy!" shouted Charlie.

"Hop aboard!" said Lulu.

And Charlie caught
his first fish.

To my fishing pole–making, boat-racing,
adventure-seeking little ones

G. P. PUTNAM'S SONS

an imprint of Penguin Random House LLC

375 Hudson Street

New York, NY 10014

Library of Congress Cataloging-in-Publication Data is available upon request.

Manufactured in China by RR Donnelley Asia Printing Solutions Ltd.

ISBN 9780399257025

1 3 5 7 9 10 8 6 4 2

Design by Annie Ericsson.
Text set in Cooper Oldstyle Light.
The art was done in watercolor with pen and ink.